Illustrated by Art Mawhinney
Adapted by Jennifer H. Keast

© 2016 Disney Enterprises, Inc. and
Pixar Animation Studios. All rights reserved.

Published by Phoenix International Publications, Inc.
7390 North Lincoln Avenue Lower Ground Floor, 59 Gloucester Place
Lincolnwood, Illinois 60712 London WIU 8JJ

p i kids is a trademark of Phoenix International Publications, Inc.,
and is registered in the United States.
Look and Find is a trademark of Phoenix International Publications, Inc.,
and is registered in the United States and Canada.

www.pikidsmedia.com

Manufactured in Canada.

8 7 6 5 4 3 2 1
ISBN: 978-1-5037-0502-9

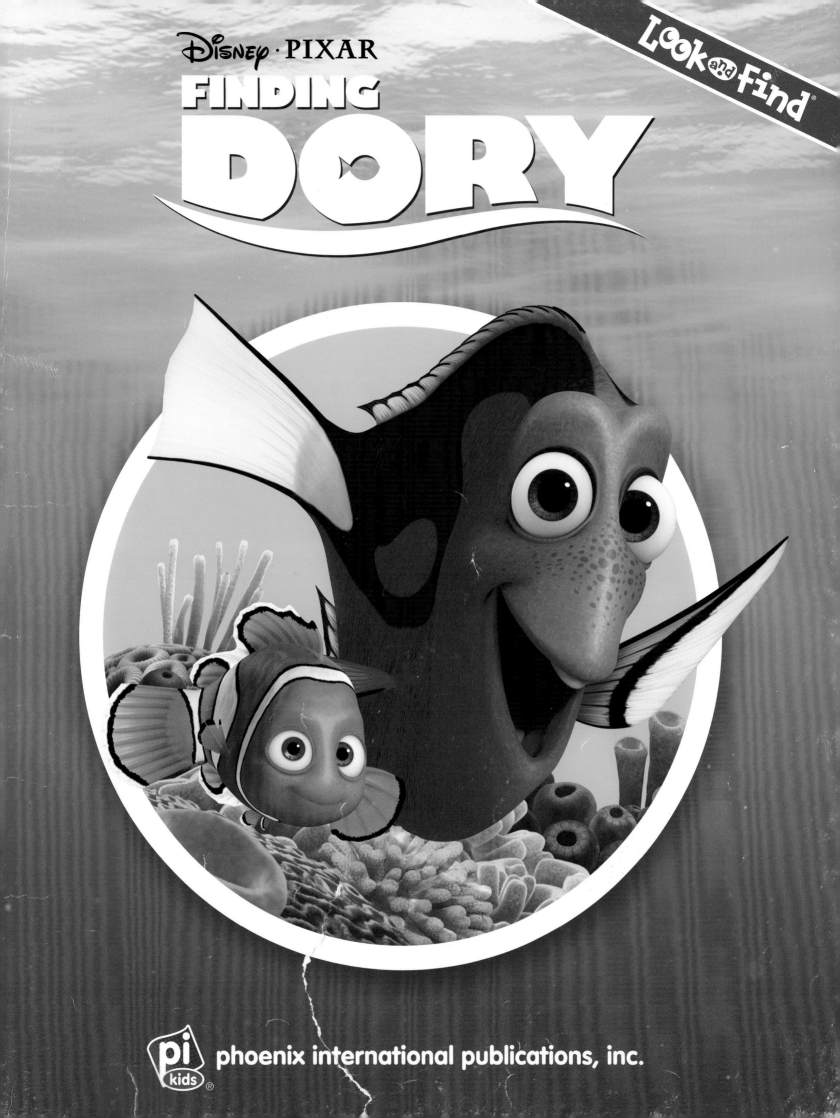

When Dory was a little fish, she lived a happy life with her parents, Jenny and Charlie...until she got swept away by the undertow.

Before she gets lost, try finding Dory, her family, and these other undersea things:

this coral

Jenny

this sea grass

Dory

the undertow

Charlie

Dory is a forgetful fish, and she doesn't remember her parents. Now Nemo and Marlin are her family. When Dory swims along on Nemo's school trip to the stingray migration, she learns that migration is about going back to where you're from.

While Dory tries to remember where *she's* from, try to spot these familiar friends:

Pearl

Nemo

Tad

Marlin

Sheldon

Mr. Ray

The migration reminds Dory that she's from California! Marlin and Nemo travel there with Dory to help her find her parents.

Can you find these underwater creatures they meet when they arrive?

Suddenly, Dory is pulled from the water by a human...and taken inside the Marine Life Institute. There, she meets an octopus named Hank, who explains that the MLI is an aquarium. Dory realizes that this is where she was born!

As Hank and Dory sneak through the staff office to search the MLI map, try searching for these aquarium-related things:

whistle

MLI tag

 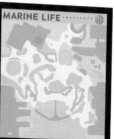

MLI map

this MLI
staff member

diving flippers

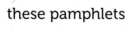

mega phone

these pamphlets

Meanwhile, Nemo and Marlin need to find a way to get to Dory. Outside the MLI, they meet some sea lions who explain that Becky the loon is the only way in.

As the clownfish hop into Becky's bucket for a ride to the MLI, look around for these things in the bay:

this loon

this otter

Becky

Rudder

this rock

Gerald

Fluke

this rock

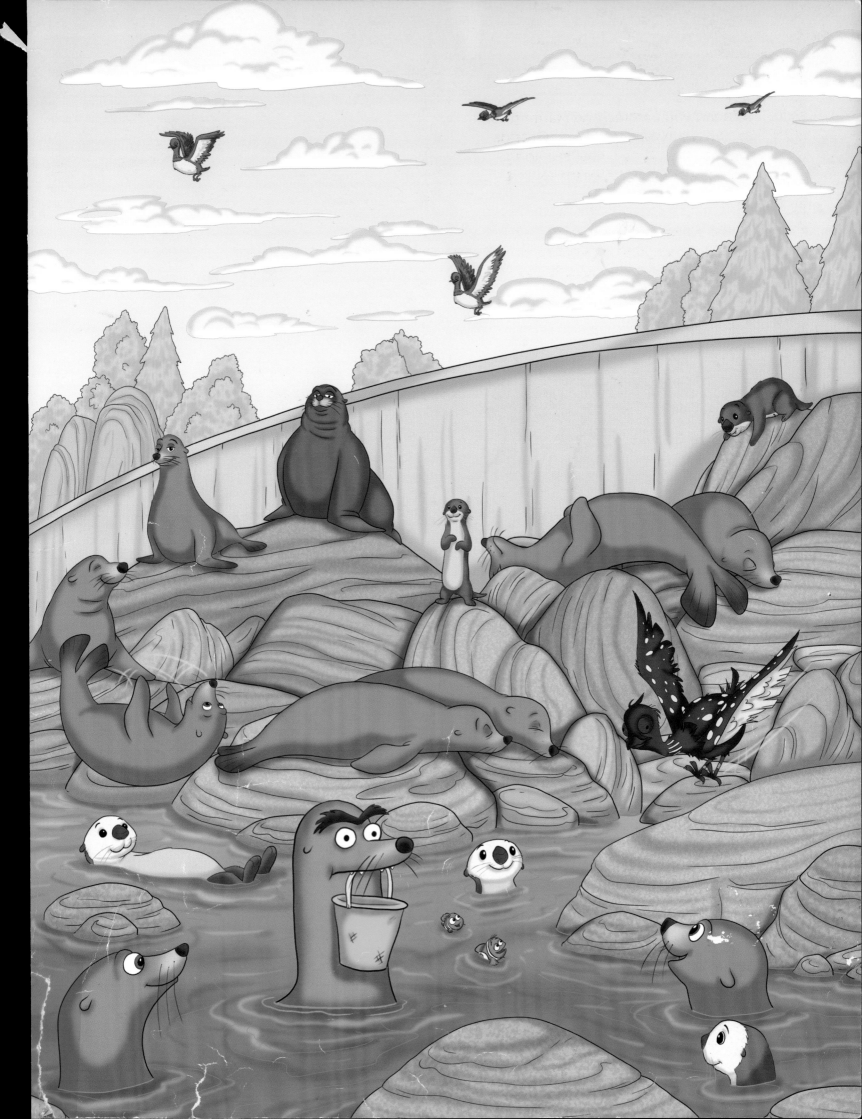

Dory ends up in a pool with a whale shark named Destiny and a beluga whale named Bailey. Destiny remembers Dory—they used to speak whale to each other through the pipes! Destiny tells Dory that she lived in the Open Ocean exhibit with her parents.

Before Hank takes Dory there, search the pool area for these new friends, old friends, and other things:

OPEN OCEAN
EXHIBIT

this sign

this pool toy

this MLI staffer

Destiny

Hank

this stroller

Bailey

When Dory finally finds the blue tangs (and Marlin and Nemo too), her parents aren't with them! It turns out Jenny and Charlie escaped to the ocean to wait for Dory to return.

As Dory thinks about this news, find these other blue tangs in the tank:

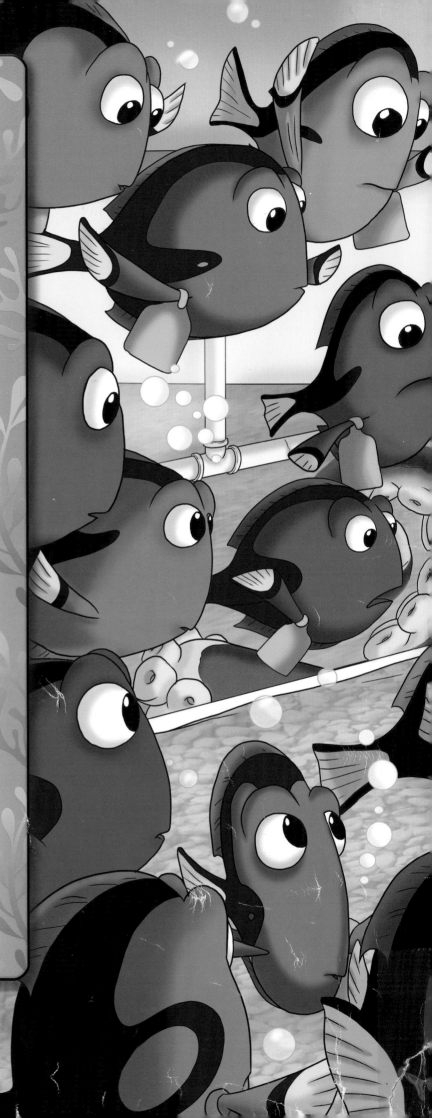

At last, Dory finds her parents in the ocean just outside the aquarium, and it's the happiest of happy endings! Now Dory lives on the reef with everyone she loves!

Join Dory's game of hide-and-seek and help her find her fun-loving family and friends:

Destiny

Bailey

Marlin

Jenny

Charlie

Pearl

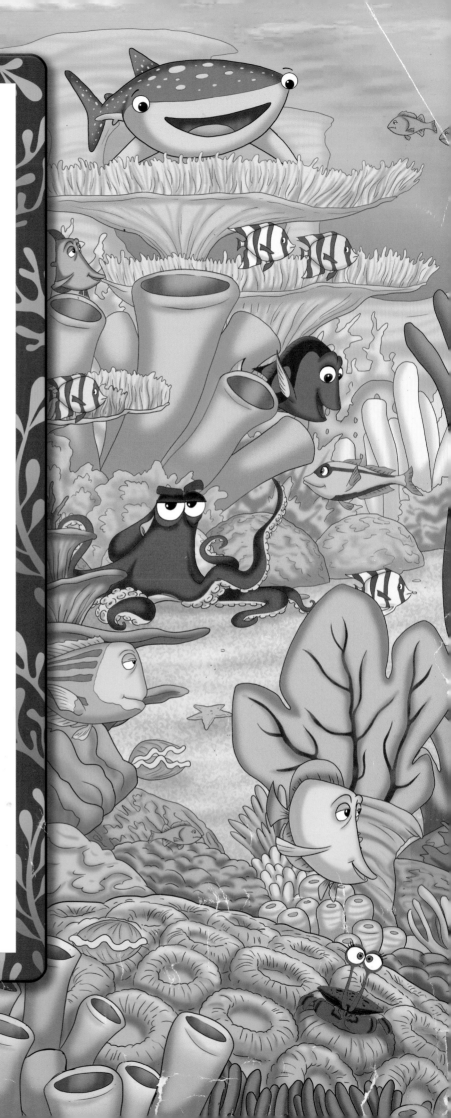

Swim back to Dory's childhood home and look for these seashells:

Migrate back to Nemo's school trip and find these stingrays on the move:

Scuttle back to the hermit crabs and look for these things that were tossed in the water:

Skip back to the MLI staff office and look for these posters:

Back up to the bay outside the aquarium and find these fishy clouds:

Pop back to the pool and find these tourists:

Trek back to the blue tang tank and look for these groups of bubbles:

Head back to the game of hide-and-seek and help Dory find these friendly faces:

this crab

this crab

Sheldon

Nemo

Hank

Tad